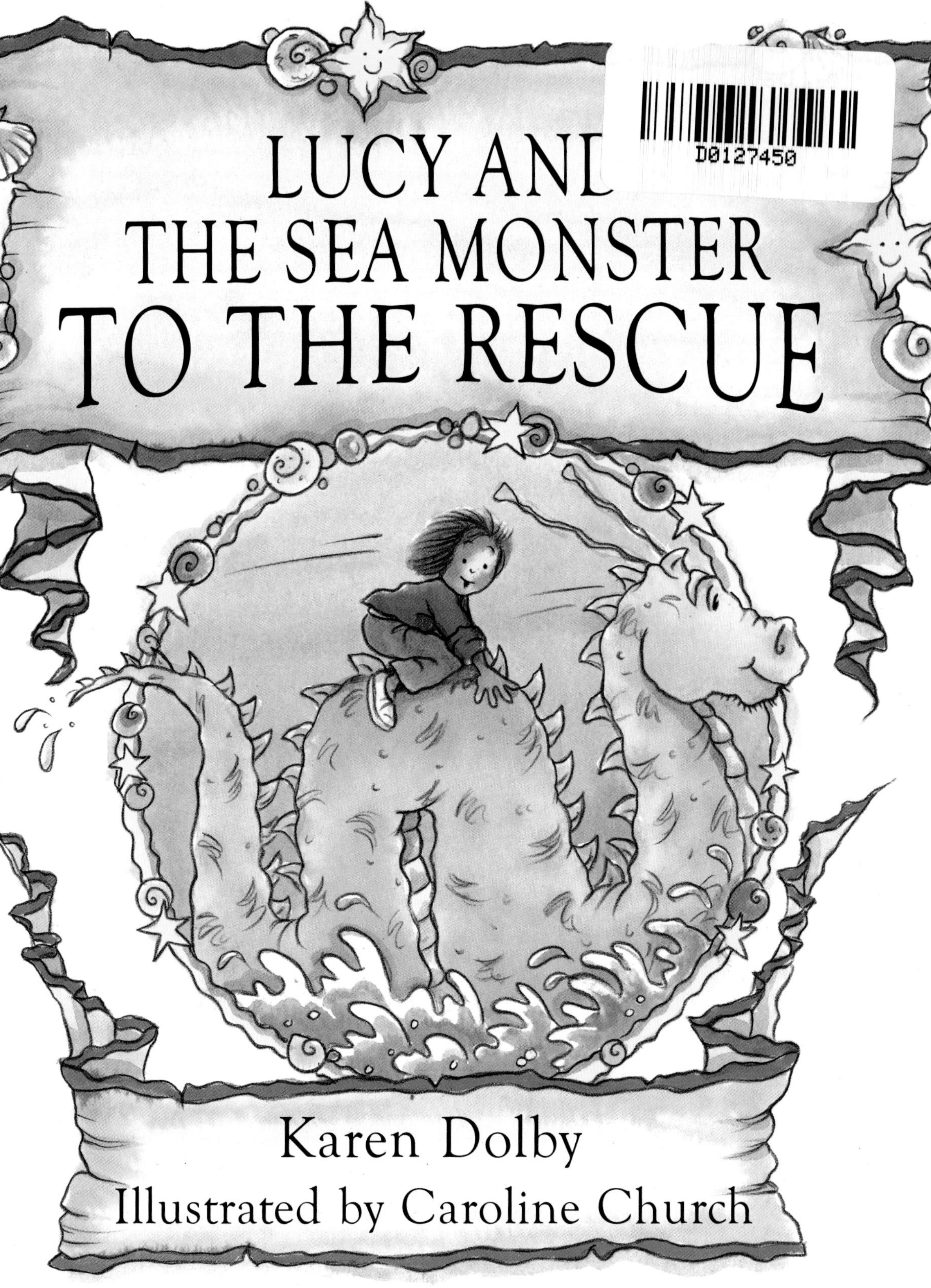

LUCY AND THE SEA MONSTER TO THE RESCUE

Karen Dolby

Illustrated by Caroline Church

Series Editor: Gaby Waters

Editor: Michelle Bates

Contents

About this Book

Lucy was scuffing through the pebbles on the beach waiting for something exciting to happen.

She did not have long to wait. When she looked up she saw a dot in the water coming closer. It was Horace, her sea monster friend.

Message in a Bottle

"Horace!" Lucy yelled, jumping up and down, waving wildly. She could hardly wait for him to reach the shore.

Horace and Lucy spent a happy morning playing hide and seek along the beach. Horace dipped and dived into rock pools, hiding below the water, then popping up again to splash Lucy unexpectedly.

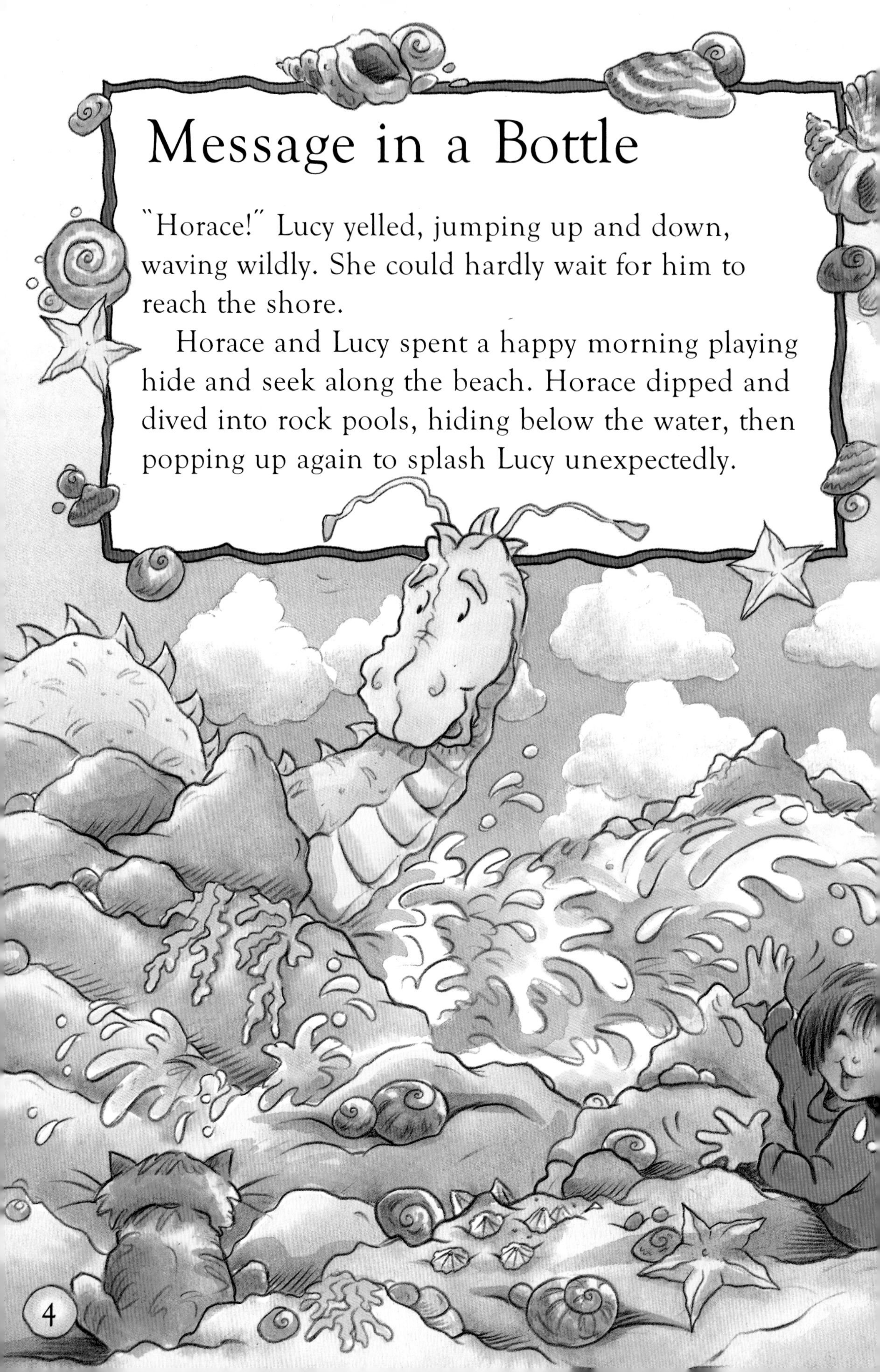

Lucy watched a large bottle bobbing up and down until a big wave flung it onto the sand at her feet. How exciting! There was a note inside. Lucy uncorked the bottle and unrolled the paper. It was a message... a message from her friends, Mel and Jim.

The Adventure Begins

"What are we waiting for? Let's go!" exclaimed Horace. Lucy scrambled onto his back and they were off.

Horace's coils sliced through the choppy sea. They whizzed along with Lucy's hair streaming behind.

Suddenly Horace stopped, so suddenly that Lucy almost fell off.

"What's wrong?" she asked.

"I'm not sure where Treasure Island is," he said. "It could be this way, that way or over there."

"We need help," said Lucy.

"You're right," said Horace. "Let's go to Neptuna, where the Merpeople live. They'll know where Treasure Island is."

Look at the signs on the rocks. Which way do you think they should go to find the Merpeople?

Which Way?

It was not long before they hit another problem. Their way was blocked.

"Oh no," sighed Lucy. "We'll never find Treasure Island or rescue Mel and Jim at this rate."

"Don't worry," said Horace. "I can see a path through the maze of rocks."

Can you find a safe way through the maze?

Neptuna

Lucy had never seen anything like Neptuna before. She rubbed her eyes to make sure she was not dreaming.

"It's market day," Horace said. "Everyone has come to do their shopping."

It was only then that Lucy noticed the floating stalls. They were piled high with shining shells, pretty pearls and coral combs; others sold fantastical fruits, fresh fish and delicious desserts.

"Let's see if anyone knows where Treasure Island is," said Lucy.

But no one did.

"Why don't you ask Rory, our roving reporter," a merman called Martin suggested. "Rory is always out and about on the lookout for news. He knows everything. He's easy to spot. He has binoculars around his neck and carries a notebook."

Can you spot Rory?

Rory's News

"Treasure Island?" said Rory, shaking his head. "Well there's good news and bad news. It's easy to spot. There are three pointed mountains, with a tree at the top of the middle one. But there's nothing to eat or drink, and it's a long way away, through the chilly Penguin Islands and beyond."

Lucy thought she had heard the bad news, but there was worse to come.

"You'd better watch out," said Rory. "Captain Silver and his pirates are heading for Treasure Island too."

Horace shivered. There was no time to lose. He knew those mean pirates only too well. They loved treasure and worst of all, kidnapped castaways to work on their ship.

Just then, Lucy glanced out to sea and spied something that made her shiver too.

What has Lucy spotted?

Penguin Islands

As the pirate ship sailed away into the distance, Lucy and Horace set off for the Penguin Islands. Penguins love ice and cold, and Lucy and Horace were about to discover just how cold and icy the islands really were. It grew chillier and chillier and as the ice lands came into view, snow began to fall.

Horace had to navigate his way between the icy islands. The penguins slid and slipped, splashing into the freezing water. But Horace was in trouble. It was hard to see through the snowflakes and even harder to steer between the jagged ice blocks, flying penguins and huge whales barring their way.

Can you find a clear route through the icy islands?

The Pirates' Lair

Horace and Lucy were happy to leave the icy Penguin Islands behind. The air grew warmer and the sun began to shine.

They swam swiftly on until they saw an island in the distance. Could this be Treasure Island? Horace was full of hope as he swam ashore, but they were in for a nasty surprise.

Not far away they heard voices and the sounds of people shouting. A horrid, burning smell filled the air. Peering through the trees Horace and Lucy spied pirates! They seemed to be squabbling about their supper.

"Yikes! This isn't Treasure Island," whispered Horace. "This is Booty Island, the pirates' base. I can see Red Reg Rover, Short Tom Gold, Black Beard and Peg Pinafore."

Can you work out which pirate is which?

Chocolate Island

Horace and Lucy didn't wait to hear more. Not wanting to be discovered, they slipped away silently.

Horace swam low in the water and Lucy lay almost flat on his back so the pirates would not spot them. They needn't have worried, the pirates were far too busy arguing to notice anything going on around them.

It was not long before a large island loomed ahead. As they drew near, the tutti-frutti trees, chocolate pebbles and a chocolate fudge stream left Lucy in no doubt. This must be the famous Chocolate Island. Lucy licked her lips as a mouthwatering smell of chocolate hit her nose.

"We could take some food and drink for Mel and Jim," said Lucy.

"But how would we carry it?" asked Horace.

Can you find something to put the food and drink in?

Lucy on the Lookout

They had soon filled their beaker and stashed all the food in the backpack. The sun was sinking low in the sky.

"We must be off," said Horace to Lucy. "I can see islands ahead. One of them must be Treasure Island. If you climb to the top of a tree you should be able to see which it is. It has three pointed mountains with a tree on top of the middle one."

Can you spot Treasure Island?

Sea Storm

No sooner had they set off, than a blustery wind began to blow. Before long it was whipping up the waves and blasting Lucy and Horace. It was hard for Lucy to keep her hold on Horace's back. The sky grew dark and menacing. Soon sharp, icy rain began to hail down on them.

"It's no good, we can't keep going," Horace yelled above the sound of the wind and waves. "We'll have to find somewhere to shelter from the storm."

Can you find a safe hiding place?

A Safe Shelter

Safe and dry in their cave, Lucy and Horace watched the rain lash down and lightning zigzag across the heavy, cloudy sky. A loud booming clap of thunder made Lucy jump but she soon spotted something which really made her heart pound.

What has Lucy seen?

There was no doubt. It was the pirates' ship and it was heading for Treasure Island. With the strong, gusting wind blowing the sails, it was speeding along. The pirates would reach the island in no time.

"What can we do?" cried Lucy. "We have to rescue Mel and Jim before the pirates arrive. There's no time to lose."

"Hop on my back," said Horace. "I have an idea."

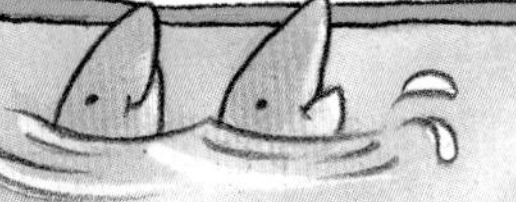

A Tricky Crossing

The wind was dropping as Lucy and Horace put to sea once more.

"Our only hope is to take the short route to Treasure Island," said Horace. "But it is tricky and very dangerous."

Can you find a way through to Treasure Island? Beware the sharp rocks, sharks, crocodiles and lurking creatures.

To the Rescue

The dangerous shortcut had been worth it. When they reached Treasure Island, Lucy looked back out to sea. There was the pirates' ship. They had beaten the greedy band.

The pirates were really quite a lazy bunch and without the wind they were having to use oars. They were rowing very slowly and singing songs about treasure and gold. They had no idea that anyone else was on the island until a shout rang out.

"Land ahoy!" the lookout yelled, pointing his telescope at the island. "Bothering barnacles! We've been beaten to the loot! Enemy ahead!"

Lucy was happy to see Mel and Jim on the shore. They were smiling, holding up a large chest. What could be inside?

Mel and Jim looked horrified as the pirates began to row frantically fast to the island.

"There's room for us all on Horace's back," Lucy called.

Before they tied on the chest, Lucy could not resist taking a peep inside. She lifted the lid. This was no ordinary treasure and certainly not the kind of gold the pirates had been expecting.

But Horace was thrilled. "It's the ancient, magical statue of Marlin! It was stolen from our underwater palace," he exclaimed. "And we thought it was lost forever."

Lucy, Mel and Jim looked puzzled, but only for a moment.

Does the statue remind you of anyone?

Homeward Bound

With the pirates in hot pursuit, Horace set off. He zipped through the water, avoiding the sharp rocks, going as fast as he dared. At last they reached clear water. But where were the pirates? Had they escaped their greedy clutches?

Lucy, Horace, Mel and Jim looked back anxiously. They had no need to fear. With their eyes on the treasure and not on the rocks, the pirates had run their boat aground. There was a large hole in it. They were angrily splashing around, squabbling loudly and blaming one another.

"I don't think they will be bothering us again," smiled Lucy as they set off for home.

Answers

Pages 6-7
Can you find the mermaid drawn on the rock? It is just behind Horace. The arrow shows which direction they should take.

Pages 8-9
The safe route through the maze is marked here.

Pages 10-11
Rory is here.

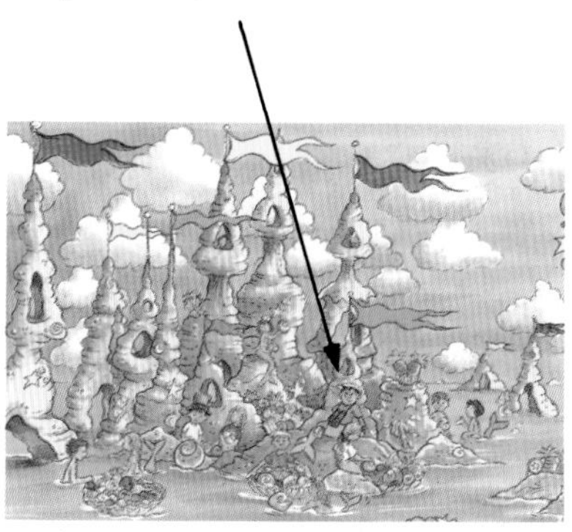

Pages 12-13
Lucy has spotted a skull and crossbones pirate flag. She is worried that this is the pirate ship Rory just told them about.

Pages 14-15
Lucy and Horace's way through the ice is shown here.

Pages 16-17
Did you guess who each pirate was from their name?

Pages 18-19
Here are the backpack and beaker.

Pages 20-21
Treasure Island is here.

Pages 22-23
They can hide in the cave circled below. It will protect them from the storm and it is the only one which does not have a creature lurking inside.

Pages 24-25
Lucy has seen the pirate flag and ship sailing on.

Pages 26-27
Their route to Treasure Island is marked here.

Pages 28-29
The treasure is a gold sea monster's head. Does it remind you of Horace?

First published in 1997 by Usborne Publishing Ltd, Usborne House, 83-85 Saffron Hill, London EC1N 8RT, England.

Printed in Portugal
First published in America March 1997. UE